IF ONLY...

MIES VAN HOUT

IF ONLY...

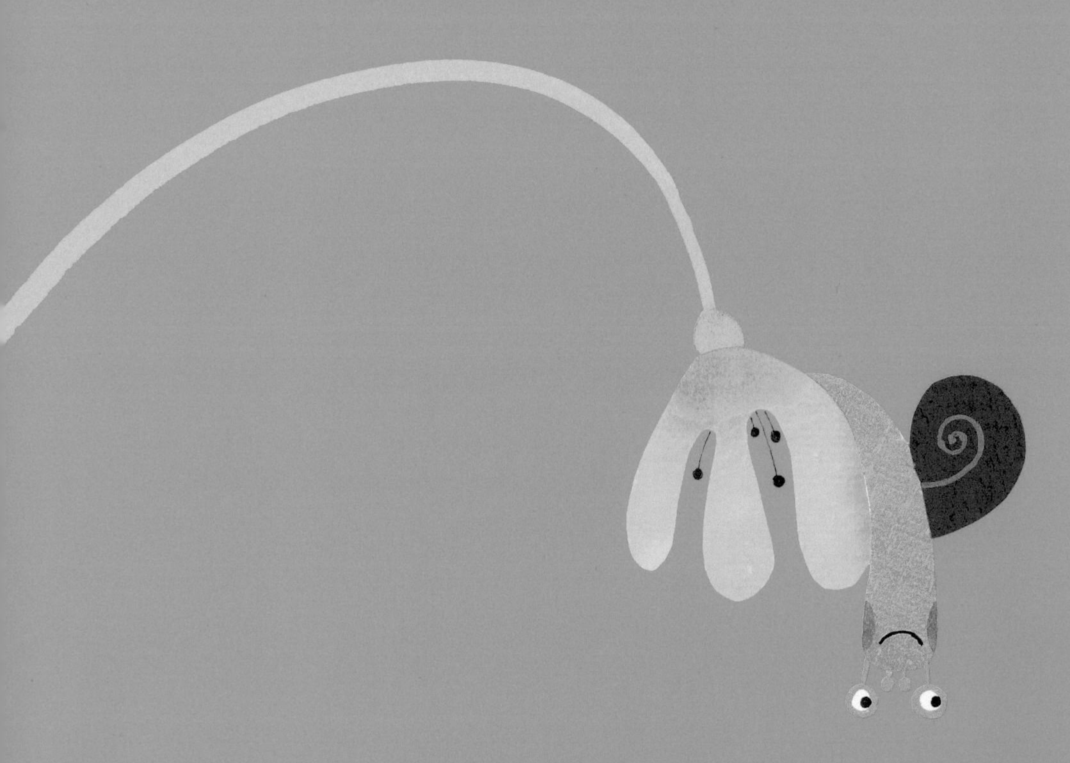

Translated by David Colmer

pajamapress

The child thought,

If only I were a butterfly.

Then I could fly everywhere.

The butterfly thought,

If only I were a stick insect.

Then I wouldn't stand out so much.

The stick insect thought,

If only I were a whirligig beetle.

Then I could swirl across the water.

The whirligig beetle thought,

If only I were a firefly.

Then I'd never be scared of the dark.

The firefly thought,
If only I were a bee.
Then I'd always have friends to help me.

The bee thought,

If only I were a spider.

Then I could do everything myself.

The spider thought,

If only I were a ladybug.

Then everyone would think I'm adorable.

The ladybug thought,

If only I were an ant.

Then I'd be strong and tough.

The ant thought,

If only I were a snail.

Then I wouldn't be this busy.

The snail thought,

If only I were a grasshopper.

Then I could jump over things.

The grasshopper thought,
If only I were a dragonfly.
Then everyone would stop to watch me go by.

The dragonfly thought,

If only I were a child.

Then I could run, jump, laugh, play hide-and-seek, count,

build houses...and so much more!

GLOSSARY OF

CREATURES

Butterflies need warm muscles to fly, so they often sit on sunny rocks or leaves with their wings spread out.

Stick insects are named for their clever camouflage: their thin brown, black, or green bodies look just like the sticks they perch on.

Whirligig beetles got their name because they swim in fast circles on the surface of the water.

Fireflies flash their lights in certain patterns to find a mate.

Bees may live in big hives like honeybees, in smaller nests like bumblebees, or alone like mason bees.

Some **spiders** use webs to catch their prey. Others jump on it from hiding or even chase it down.

Ladybugs are cute, but their babies are not! These long, black, scaly-looking larvae are helpful garden defenders that eat pests.

Depending on its species, an **ant** can carry objects from 10 to 50 times its own weight. A few can carry even more!

Some **snails** live in water, but they cannot swim. They crawl on a trail of mucus just like land snails.

Grasshoppers use their big back legs like catapults to launch themselves into the air.

Dragonflies have some fancy tricks. They can fly upside down or backward and can turn a full circle in the air. They also eat mosquitoes!

MAKE COLLAGE ART LIKE

MIES VAN HOUT

In this book, each creature wants to be like one of the others. What creature would you like to be? What is something they can do that you can't?

Follow these steps to make a collage of your creature.

WHAT YOU NEED

- a large piece of paper
- scraps of colored paper
- self-painted paper (see inset)
- old magazines
- markers or crayons
- scissors
- glue

COLLAGE YOUR CREATURE

Start with a big sheet of white or colored paper for your base. Collect scraps of craft paper, newspapers, wallpaper, and magazines. You can also paint on plain paper to make your own colorful scraps (see inset).

Cut or tear shapes from the colored paper and lay them on your base sheet.

Move the pieces around until they look like your creature. Do you have enough scraps? Do you have too many?

If you don't like one scrap, put it aside and look for one that fits better.

Slide all your scraps around and rearrange them until you're happy.

Glue all the pieces in place.

Finish your art with markers or crayons

When the glue is dry, you can finish your collage by drawing on details. Use markers or crayons to draw features like a mouth, legs, and eyes.

Have fun!

Making self-painted paper

What you need

- white paper
- sponge
- colored ink
- brushes
- paper towel
- water
- newspaper

Create self-painted paper for your collage

Using a sponge, wet a white sheet of paper on both sides.

Lay the sheet on a table and make sure it is smooth.

Pat the sheet with a paper towel, but don't dry it completely.

Paint on the wet paper with colored ink.

The ink will make spreading blots on the wet paper. The wetter the paper, the wider the blots will be.

Leave the sheet on some newspaper to dry.

First published in Canada and the United States in 2021

Originally published by Uitgeverij Hoogland & Van Klaveren, Hoorn, the Netherlands under the title *Was ik maar...*

Translation rights arranged by élami agency

10 9 8 7 6 5 4 3 2 1

www.pajamapress.ca info@pajamapress.ca

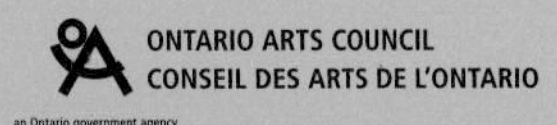

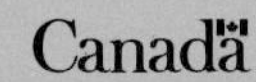

The publisher gratefully acknowledges the support of the Canada Council for the Arts and the Ontario Arts Council for its publishing program. We acknowledge the financial support of the Government of Canada through the Canada Book Fund (CBF) for our publishing activities.

Library and Archives Canada Cataloguing in Publication
Title: If only... / Mies van Hout ; translated by David Colmer.
Other titles: Was ik maar... English
Names: Hout, Mies van, author. | Colmer, David, 1960- translator.
Description: First North American edition. | Translation of: Was ik maar...
Identifiers: Canadiana 20200411020 | ISBN 9781772781960 (hardcover)
Classification: LCC PZ7.H8325 If 2021 | DDC j839.313/7–dc23

Publisher Cataloging-in-Publication Data (U.S.)
Names: Hout, Mies van, author, illustrator. | Colmer, David 1960-, translator
Title: If only... / Mies Van Hout ; translated by David Colmer.
Description: Toronto, Ontario Canada : Pajama Press, 2020. | Previously published by Hoogland & Van Klaveren , Haarlem, Netherlands as Was ik maar... | Summary: "In a cyclical story, a child wishes to fly like a butterfly, who wishes for privacy like a stick insect's, who wishes to swim like a whirligig beetle. Each garden creature expresses a desire to be like someone else, ending with the dragonfly who wants to be like a child who can run, jump, laugh, play, count, build, and more" -- Provided by publisher.
Identifiers: ISBN 978-1-77278-196-0 (hardcover)
Subjects: LCSH: Human behavior - Juvenile fiction. | Animals -- Adaptation - Juvenile fiction. | Envy - Juvenile fiction. | BISAC: JUVENILE FICTION / Social Themes / Self-Esteem & Self-Reliance. | JUVENILE FICTION / Social Themes / Emotions & Feelings.
Classification: LCC PZ7.H688If |DDC [E] - dc23

Original art created with acryl-ink, gouache and collage
Cover and book design–Lorena González Guillén

Manufactured in China by WKT Company

Pajama Press Inc.
469 Richmond St. E, Toronto, ON M5A 1R1

Distributed in Canada by UTP Distribution
5201 Dufferin Street Toronto, Ontario Canada, M3H 5T8

Distributed in the U.S. by Ingram Publisher Services
1 Ingram Blvd. La Vergne, TN 37086, USA